FOUR DIAMONDS IN THE ROUGH

by

C. Bailey-Cassell

The purpose of this book is to inform and entertain. The author has attempted to recreate events, locales and conversations as best from her memories of them.

Author: C. Bailey-Cassell

ISBN 978-0-244-15158-4

Acknowledgements

A huge thank you to my mother, Sharon Bailey, who introduced me to the world of books in our local library; where I not only found my love for reading but also the inspiration to create my own stories. I love you Mum!

Thank you to my aunty, Lorraine Phillips, an incredible writer in her own right and my personal inspiration...who encouraged me to just step out and get it done!

Thank you also to my friends and those who have supported this journey, to name a few: Christelle, Diana, Ronnie, Jordan, Ray, Kelly, Obatare, Chanessa, Vanessa, Esther, Kodjo, Mondz, Joey and Sherene for believing in me and taking time out to read my extracts and short stories over the years.

To Dad, Herman Cassell, I love and miss you and hope you are proud of me.

To Rita and Gill, diamonds in their own right. For their time and investing me to strive for something greater.

To Aaron (AaronJamespoet), Asser (ahumblefella) and Karim (Karimpoetry) my fellow writers, for their advice and support.

Shout-out to my illustrator, Creativesellu for the fantastic illustrations of these beautiful women.

And finally, to God, my Saviour, for gifting me with this talent for writing, instilling in me a creative mind and imagination and forming the words of which I write.

Love you all, C x

Introduction

Each one of the four girls were very different. Different in the way they looked, the way they spoke and in the way they behaved. I couldn't have imaged that they were from the same world as one another, as each one saw the world in completely dissimilar ways from one another.

Each girl gave me their version of events of that dreadful night and the events which led up to it. Had I not known that it was the same night they were talking about, I would not have believed otherwise.

They had been referred to me for counselling as a result of their terrible ordeals. Each girl had suffered post-traumatic stress, though they would not agree, but were offered the service as a form of outlet.
For obvious reasons, I cannot release their actual names. Instead, I have made up names for them which I feel go not only go with their characters, but also fits them as a description.

China Rhea Redson

The first girl came in to see me. I could tell from the moment she walked through the door, that she was a fiery character. Confident. She didn't appear to really care about anything or anyone but herself; that was the gist I acquired from the first conversation we had.
As she sat down and looked around my office, judging it by her own standards, I noticed this arrogant and ever-so bossy air about her.

"I don't really understand why I'm here. I don't feel as though what happened has affected me at all, to be honest. And I know that sounds really bad, as he was my boyfriend and I did love him and all

of that, but he wasn't really the love of my life. I guess I am a little bit sad, but not enough to need counselling about it. I think this is all too much." She said aggressively.

Everything about her was very much, *'me, myself and I'*. An attitude which seemed to soak every sentence she ever said in the sessions I had with her. Everything either, started with her, became about her or ended with her.

"Okay, so you don't really know why you're here. Maybe then we can talk a bit about what happened and see if that helps?"

She wasn't too keen on that idea. It was as if I was taking up way too much of her time and energy. It was clear that she had better things to be doing; shopping, working or both.

"Oh," She began, already exhausted from the thought of having to discuss anything, *"Do you not already know what happened?"*

"I know parts, but I would like to hear about what happened from your viewpoint."

"Oh, okay."

I could tell I had gripped her into a conversation by simply making 'her' the most important thing in the situation. In her eyes, I was highly interested in 'her' and in her description of the whole night never mind anything else; those were simply 'minor' details.

I decided to call her: China Rhea Redson.

Phoebe Roberts

Then there was Phoebe. Phoebe Roberts, we'll call her. She was in stark contrast to China, laidback, calm, composed. She was someone you could sit in a room with, just you and her, and feel comfortable sitting in complete silence. Surrounded by her peaceful nature and tranquil disposition, you could almost forget she was even there with you if you took your mind off her for a moment.

She was a pleasant girl but it was quite difficult to get her motivated to talk about what she was thinking or feeling. There was a lot of digging to be done with this one. She didn't give me much, with or without me asking her. But it wasn't as though she wanted to hold back information from me deliberately; it was more as though she was worried about what I would say about what she had to say, or I could go as far to say, that she simply could not be bothered to talk about it.

Her version of events, were at the opposite end of the spectrum to China's, a whole different perspective completely. It was hard to believe they were at the same place at the same time with the same people.

Robyn McKenzie

I could not get a full picture from both China and Phoebe of what happened of that night, but I didn't need to because there was Robyn. Robyn McKenzie. She gave me all that I needed and more in terms of vivid detail about the night in question. Her level of insight and perspective allowed me to see things in a light that I could have not imagined them in. She cleverly helped me to piece together the missing pieces of the puzzle that filled that night with her creative, intellectual, analytical and reflective mind. I could see from the way she told me certain details which happened on that night, that she had spent time thinking how each little detail leading up to it had caused a major effect on what had happened.

However, I could also see the damage that this thinking had done to her emotional side. She, out of all of the girls, was the most depressed. I wasn't sure whether that was more to do with who she was in this whole saga, if that was just the cause of over-thinking or whether it was both. But I found it unpleasant to watch; especially as with each session, it tended to get progressively worse.

Thankfully, though, she ended up feeling much better having gotten it out of her system as I found out when our sessions came to a close.

Cyan Imogen Brown

Cyan was as colourful as her name. Last but by no means the less vibrant character I've ever met. Her presence literally lit up my office like sunshine pouring into a room - that was Cyan. She was chatty, spontaneous and appeared to be extremely fun. Although she was a conversationalist, and was way more of a storyteller than any of the other girls combined, her stories were terribly hard to follow. She may as well have never said anything in the first place; nothing literally really made that much sense.

Her conversations were about as disorganised as her life. Not only that but she was highly forgetful. If something hadn't interested her or wasn't about her, she couldn't remember it actually happening and so often left it out of the conversation. But then I suppose that was because she very much lived in the present moment. She wasn't too much concerned about the events of that morning, let alone yesterday, and was far too busy enjoying the here and now to be concerned with what 'had' happened.

The only real reason I was able to get so much out of her about what had happened was because, not only did she love talking, she also loved the fact that she was getting attention for her story; as exaggerated as it often was.

China Rhea Redson

She started from her beginning of things, which I later found out wasn't actually the real beginning - only she didn't know that. When she spoke, it was as though each word had a disgusting taste in her mouth and the only way she could get rid of the word was by spitting each word out; especially when she spoke about him...

"It was just another one of those parties he had told me to come to." She said hurriedly, as though that wasn't an important factor in the story.

"Who is 'he'?" I asked realising that talking to China was probably going to require more energy on my part; largely due to her talking as though whoever she's speaking to, was supposed to know 'who' and 'what' she was talking about without her having to say so.

"Oh sorry," She said apologetically, *"My boyfriend."* She informed me before continuing with what she had been saying before I cut her off.

But I wasn't interested in what she was saying at the end of the sentence. I was much more interested in how she *felt* in general about him requesting her presence at functions; it didn't seem the least bit nice.

"Tell me a bit about your relationship with him?" I questioned her.

Watching as she sat, legs crossed in a short, bright, red dress which not only showed off her curves but left nothing for the imagination. She had entered my office as though she was entering into a fashion show, no more so as though she was a running for a 'Miss London' beauty pageant. Yes, she was an extremely beautiful young lady, but by God, she knew it! Holding enough confidence in herself and her looks for two people. I could tell that she had a presence about her which would make many others feel extremely intimidated just by her simply walking past them. She acted like a boss and spoke like one too! She clearly didn't appreciate being cut off, or even being questioned, but she didn't have much choice in the matter as that was my job to ask her about herself and I suppose that was why she continued to come and see me.

"Him...hmmm. He was nice I guess, not really my type, in terms of looks, but he gave me everything I wanted and needed so of course, he was a keeper. Nice height I guess, good build..."

"What about his character, his personality?"

"Erm, he was funny a bit, didn't talk much, not to me anyway..."

Because you did enough talking for the both of you, I thought to myself.

"...He was considerate, kind, gentle. Made time for me, whenever I needed him, he was there."

"What about when he needed you? Would you say that you made time for him?"

She took a while to think about the answer to my question, but I knew the answer before she even said it.

"I definitely made time for him."

"Okay, I don't mean when it was just convenient for you, I mean at times when he needed you and you weren't totally available; if there were times like that, would you say that you made an effort to see him?"

"No." She said matter-of-factly.

I wasn't surprised. This formed the basis of my future questions regarding him. I had to get her to realise that he was a person with his own thoughts, behaviours and characteristics besides her. I had to break down their relationship in order for her to see him for who he was to her.

I moved onto questions of that night to build up a picture of her world in my own head.

"Okay China, I want you to tell me as much as you can remember from that night, from beginning to end." I knew it was going to be mostly about herself but there was a lot that I could infer from even the little things that she told me.

"He came to get me at around 9 pm, I hadn't finished getting ready so he had to wait a while...I'd say about, 45 mins. I told him that I could make my own way. Meet him there - I drove too but he liked having me on his arm; like I was some trophy or something. Not that I complained, when you look as good as me you get that kind of treatment! But yeah, he wasn't mad. He was used to it by now, we'd been together something like 3 or 4years and he knew it took me a while to look good and on a night where all of our people were going to be at, I had to make even more of an effort to look good.

I remember getting into the passenger seat of his car and his reaction was, "Damn baby, you look fine!" in his dumb American accent he liked to put on from time to time. I hated it. Loved the attention and the compliments but hated the accent, as I constantly told him. Did he listen? No! But anyway...We must have got to the house party at 11 pm. I remember fixing my make-up on the journey. He was talking to me on the drive but I wasn't really paying attention to what he was saying, his conversation sometimes bored me. We got there now, he came around my side, to open my door after he'd parked up - I never liked to open my own door, that was one thing I didn't do, especially since I had so much to carry, my LV bag and my Burberry coat - not that I really wanted to carry my coat there, didn't like to take expensive things to places like that, never know whose hands were feeling light..."

She babbled on about the journey to the house and what she was thinking in regards to the house, etc. until I asked her about whose house it was.

"Oh I don't know, one of his friends I think."

"So he didn't tell you the occasion of the party or who was going...?" I tried reaching out for answers to questions I thought she would have known the answers to.

"He probably did, I don't know. You need to know that after a while, I just stopped listening to him regarding certain details, well, things I felt were trivial to me. All I needed to know was that there was a party happening that he wanted me, as his girlfriend, to go with him to and I had to dress up and look the part basically."

She looked at me with her hand stretched out towards me, as though what she had just said was sitting in the palm of her hand and she was offering it to me.

"Okay, so tell me about the course of the night."

"There were a lot of people in there already, even though it was relatively early. Usually, people don't start arriving till 12 am, but anyway, I saw faces I didn't recognise but who recognised me. People trying to say hello to me as though we went way back but I'm there looking in their faces like I've literally just seen them for the first time. I'm not rude though, I'll say hello back even though I don't know you, just don't expect me to make conversation with

you. I remember being around the guys in the kitchen, I went there to get myself a drink but in all honesty that was where the hot guys were. I introduced myself to them and basically spent the evening in their company. Can't remember their names though, I think one was called...something beginning with T...don't know but he was nice, gosh. There were three of them.
Anyway, so I'm basically with them, and then I hear a scream from the main room where the party is happening. We just think some silly girl has been knocked over or something so we just ignore it but then I see the light go on from the hallway and the music stopped. Then we just hear lots of screaming. I need to go see what's happening so I go in there and see a whole load of people fighting and someone on the floor. I'm there trying to get past the guys and girls fighting and see who is on the floor but everyone is being pushed and I can't get to them. Then suddenly, I get picked up from behind and carried outside."

She giggles a little bit, which makes me feel comfortable as the result of her story is not something to be laughing about. I know she's laughing because of a funny memory, though, it is not totally clear why it was funny but as the conversation continues, I realise why.

"Who carried you outside?"

"Tyrone."

"And who's Tyrone?"

"A guy that I've been kinda seeing..."

"Kind of seeing?"

"Yeah, sort of was messing with."

I didn't need to ask anything else to know that she had been cheating with this, Tyrone guy, on her boyfriend. But why had he carried her out at that time? With what had just happened at that specific moment in time, was a mystery to me but one that I wanted to find the answer to.

Robyn McKenzie

Enter in next. Robyn.

Robyn seemed like a lovely girl on first impression. She had walked into my office with such a brilliant smile, one that masked her sadness so well. My initial thoughts about her were that she was a quiet one, one that was difficult to communicate with. I was very wrong. If anything I found her the easiest to communicate with, although she wouldn't agree. She always seemed to be worried whether I understood what she had said or if it made sense. Asking, "Does that make sense?" as a sub-clause, to almost everything she ever said. I'm exaggerating slightly, but though she didn't come across as totally sure of herself, there was something about the way she spoke about things. As though she had spent time going over things in her mind and cross-referencing with other factors about the things she had seen and therefore learnt about herself and the others...

"Hello, Robyn. How are you?"

"Okay, I guess." She replied with a slight smile.

I could tell that was her effort to be friendly, although she came across highly troubled about her recent experience.

"Any emotion you feel in this office is okay to be expressed. I want you to know that if you feel like crying you can and if you feel like being angry - that too is fine, as long as that anger is not expressed physically!" I joked. But her girly giggle told me that, not only did that help make her feel more comfortable but also that I wouldn't have to worry too much about her becoming violent. On the contrary, her tears were my biggest concern.

“We can start with you telling me about that night or we can start with your relationship with him. It’s totally up to you.” I told her, careful to space my words as I could see, from her blank expression, that she wasn’t totally in the room. I was intrigued to know what flashback had grabbed her or what was occupying her attention but I didn't have to wait too long to find out.

“I think I loved him. No. I know that I did.”

I knew who she was talking about but I needed to clarify, just in case it wasn’t who I thought she was talking about.

“Are we talking about him?”

“Yes.” She said, looking at me dead in the eye.

Cyan Imogen Brown

Cyan startled me when she first entered my office. She came in with a flood of tears. In no way was she crying silently either. It was as though the event had just happened as opposed to the actual week ago it had been.

As she sat down, I handed her a box of tissues. Taking one, she blew into it furiously.
I sat still watching her wondering if it was too soon for her to be talking about what had happened, but I was wrong. As soon as she got herself together, which didn't take long, it was as though she had put on a whole new persona.

"Okay, I'm ready! Apologies for my emotions, I'm really trying to keep it together but it's so difficult. He meant so much to me you know, like I can't actually believe what's happened. Today he was meant to be following me to the studio so I could work on my new song, and now obviously that can't happen!" And her emotions took hold of her once again.

I took this opportunity to ask a question. I could see quite clearly it was going to be difficult for me to be able to get a word in edgeways; she was a talker!

"You say he meant so much to you. Tell me a bit about your relationship with him." I said softly. I wondered if I should have used 'briefly' in my sentence but thought it would probably be ignored anyway.

"Yeah, he did. No one will get our relationship. He was life! He was like a brother to me...well nah, that's weird. But that's how it started. I met him through China – that's my girl from school. She's

my 'ride or die'. They were together and so we got close through her. We were like a trio. But he and I sort of clicked. I don't know any other way to put it. Like, he was into music as I was. He was a producer and I wanted to sing so he'd tell me to come to the studio where he used to work and we'd just mess around with a couple beats and just buss joke. Like, he got my humour. We would sit together for hours and just laugh. And yeah I found him attractive, how could you not find him attractive? I know that's why China stayed with him for so long. He was the sexiest guy we knew. Everyone wanted him. But I know why he went for China, she's pretty, I know. But they didn't click like we did. I think that's why..."

Eventually, she stopped, well hesitated. I could tell that she was about to say something quite important but had remembered herself and how much she was sharing. Although I was relieved she had paused - thankful for the brief silence - I desperately wanted her to continue her point.

"Everything you say here stays here. I just want you to remember that Cyan. And you are not obliged to share anything you don't want to." I informed her, but I really wanted her to be as open as she had been.

She looked at me, smiled her lovely smile and continued. *"I think that's why we started messing around together."* She looked at me to see my reaction. But I was trained for this. Give nothing away in your expression; constant poker face.

"Yeah, we acted on our attraction towards one another."

"Did China know?" I asked, treading carefully.

"Nah," She laughed, *"Not that she would have cared anyway. I think that was part of the fun. Having something you know you shouldn't have. It was spontaneous, it wasn't planned. He dropped*

me home after we had spent all night in the studio and I just thought, life is too short, and kissed him. He kissed me back and it started from there. We both knew what it was. I wasn't stupid. Whenever I wanted him, I got him and it was made easy the fact that we both had an excuse to be together. China never suspected anything. She thought we just did music together. She had no idea the type of music we were literally making!"

She laughed at her own dry pun, slapping her thigh and leaning back in her chair to get more comfortable. Not that she could really sit still. She had been moving around in some kind of capacity while she had been telling her story.

"So what I'm hearing is that you and he had a sexual relationship or an 'arrangement' outside of the relationship he had with China, that China knew nothing about?"

"Yes, we were...how would I put it...?" She began, her mind searching for a way to describe it but I could see she was having trouble.

"Friends with benefits?" I tried.

"Yeah, I like that. You could say that's what we were. I remember this one time..."

I listened to her tell yet another story of one of their many rendezvous together, whilst thinking about how emotionally volatile she was. Crying one minute at a sad memory and then weeping tears of laughter at a memory she enjoyed with him. I don't know how accurate any of the details were in her stories but they were indeed colourful!

Phoebe Roberts

Phoebe was different. It was quite clear in our first conversation that she wasn't a part of China and Cyan's world. In fact, I don't even think she knew of them, which I found incredibly strange. I decided against telling her about his 'other' life. I wanted to get as much out of her as possible and didn't want anything I told her to affect anything she was willing to tell me.
I asked her a bit about herself.

"I'm 21, I work as an administrator in a GP practice, erm...I don't know, what else you want to know?"

I was focusing on her body language as she was talking. She had made herself right at home. If she'd leant back anymore on the chair, she'd be lying down! She looked as snug as a bug sitting there, as though she'd been there for ages. So comfortable and at brilliant ease. She made me feel calm just looking at her. However, it was hard to get things out of her. She didn't talk much, it was difficult to get her motivated to talk about the events and how she was feeling about all that happened.

"So what was your relationship to him?"

"We were seeing each other." She said without much emotion.

I was curious as to how this relationship worked, on account of how many relationships he clearly had on the go. China, I know was probably the person he saw the least. She made it seem as though she had no real time for him and that they only saw one another when she was free, or he had invited her somewhere which wasn't often.

Cyan, on the other hand, made it seem like they were together all the time. Had she been exaggerating? More than likely, but still, it was odd that neither of the girls suspected him to be seeing anyone else more than what they did know. I decided not to ask any questions about it just in case.

"So tell me a bit about your relationship - when did you see him? Spend time with him? Tell me a bit about how he treated you, etc."

"Erm," She began, blowing out air as though what I was had asked of her was a major task that would take so much energy.

"We spoke mostly on the phone when he had time. He was usually busy at the studio so he came to see me when he could. I had no problems with that. I knew he wasn't lying. I always heard his music in the background when he would call to check on me. He was a busy guy. I liked that. He wasn't jobless like half of these guys these days. I had to respect his hustle. Plus, I'm not really that kind of girl who needs to see you all the time or really stresses him to spend time with me. I was cool with seeing him as and when. He told me that I was his peace. I liked that."

"How did you two meet?"

"I was out one day and he approached me and asked for my number. He was good-looking, I was single and so I gave it to him. We started talking from that day on."

"How long ago was this?"

"3 months ago now."

"How did you feel about him?"

"I loved him. He was my everything."

"Did anyone know about him?"

"I didn't tell my family at first about him. Especially, my brother, he's quite overprotective of me even though he's like a year older than me. I'm not really someone who announces their business either, but I just wanted to keep it to myself anyway."

I took her answer for a 'no'.

Robyn McKenzie

I'd be honest. I'm biased. Robyn was my favourite one of the girls to speak to. She gave me as much information as I needed and her relationship with 'him' was such that I got a wide perspective on his life. Still, I could see she was holding something back. She was his best friend or 'bestie', as she called it. They were apparently very close but there was something about this closeness that she wasn't happy with...

"We went school together. I was the one he'd copy from in class. He got straight A's because of me. But I don't know. I don't think I was his type or something. I was okay with that, at first. There were so many girls who liked him but he didn't give the time of day to so I suppose back then, being his best friend was better than nothing."

"So I assume, you being his best friend meant that he confided in you about all of his relationships?" I asked, trying not to be too presumptuous, but she could tell from my facial expression that I knew what she also knew.

She looked down at her feet and I could see her thinking how to put it.

"Yeah, I knew about them."

"Who is 'them'?" I asked for clarity, just in case she wasn't aware of as many of the girls as I was; which of course was silly to think, if anything she'd know more.

"China, Cyan and another one, he never told me her name or what she looked like or anything, said I didn't need to know. He'd still tell me about her though. Not that there was ever much to tell. From

what he told me she sounded boring, I don't even know why he was messing with her really."

I wanted to say it was because she was his 'peace' but decided against it. The way she was talking sounded like she wouldn't have reacted well to that comment anyway. She was coming across in a highly emotional way; however, I couldn't place what type of emotion she was expressing. I listened as she continued to give me her break-down of all three of the girls.

"...So yeah I didn't care to know much about that one. She was irrelevant to me, to be honest. I was more concerned with China and Cyan." Her brows fused together as she said their names.

Then it hit me. What that emotion was in her voice. Envy. She had feelings for him and envied these girls. I didn't say anything as I felt a vent coming on and I knew she was about to release a critique of both females.

"China thinks she's too nice. I mean yeah she's pretty; yeah she's independent and has it all together literally. But she treated him like he wasn't worthy of her. I don't know why he had her on such a high pedestal. She didn't deserve him. I think I met her once and she was just so rude. Like you know when you meet someone and they clearly don't like you but they talk to you to be civil. Some know-it-all as well. I didn't like that, trying to tell me things about him as though I didn't know him. And boy was she controlling. She'd summon him whenever she felt like it and demanded so much of him. I would say she had him whipped but he was messing with other girls too so I don't think she had him that whipped..."

I was tempted to cut in here and ask why it was, she thought, he was cheating on her. But I was too into her take on each of the girls and so didn't want to stop her flow.

"...Cyan. Pfff. Her 'friend' you know. He begged me to keep that quiet; which I did. But it burned me every time he spoke about her, like they were best friends. I hated that. More than I hated the way China used to treat him. He was MY best friend but it was like they had more 'sexual chemistry' or something. I guess that's what he meant, but I think to her, he was her 'bestie'." She said, rolling her eyes.

Robyn sighed. I could tell getting it out of her system was helping her somewhat and I found it incredibly fascinating.

How I wished I could speak to him myself and hear first-hand how he managed all four girls and how he regarded each one! Robyn was doing a good job of analysing, but how much did she really know? I mean she barely knew much about Phoebe, but how much was she actually letting on?

I hadn't thought about it before but I began to wonder if any of the girls had anything to hide. I was certain that at least one of these girls had some part to play in his death, but who and how?

China Rhea Redson

"So China, tell me about this 'Tyrone'. We finished our session last time with your admission that you had been having a secret relationship on the side."

I crossed my legs and sat back waiting while she applied the finishing touches to her lipstick and placed it back in her pristine LV bag. I didn't know for what reason she had to put on lipstick, there was no one in here to impress.

"He's just got the full package really. Handsome, ambitious, great body, great..." She blushed and licked her lips at the same time. I didn't have to be a genius to get what she was implicitly implying.

"Tell me a bit about his character, or how he is with you. Did he know you were in a relationship?"

"His character...hmm, I guess he's the strong silent type. The one thing I like about him is that he is his own man. He doesn't let me boss him around."

Again, where have I heard her say this before? I thought to myself.

"He lets me do my own thing and although he doesn't treat me like a Queen, well how I like to be treated, there is something about him that makes me want to come back for more. He's never tried to hold me down or demand me to be his girl. It's almost like he doesn't want me...it's quite sexy. Yeah, he knew I was in a relationship. Everyone knew! I didn't keep that a secret. In fact, that's the first thing I told him when we met. 'I have a man sorry'. But he didn't even approach me like that."

"So how did you to meet?"

"Funny story,"

I was certain it wasn't going to be all that funny, but I leaned forward to show my interest all the same.

"I met him at the gym. I had just arrived and was making my way towards one of the treadmills. Before I could get on it, he was already in my face. Sweat glistening on his squared, freshly trimmed brow, I could smell the coconut oil from where I was standing and that wasn't too far away from him. His body was so defined and muscular. I like my guys big. Anyway, he began with, 'Hi," and immediately I thought to myself, you're so hot but I'm taken. And so I told him so. He laughed. I remember that because I got angry, I thought he was trying to say that there was something wrong with me, that it was unbelievable or inconceivable for me to have someone. I brushed him off and proceeded to walk but that was difficult because he was still standing in my way. I told him to move, rudely. He stopped laughing and looked at me, like I had just offended him or something. Raising his eyebrows he said, 'kool' and stepped to the side. I kissed my teeth under my breath because he wasn't too far away from me, and I got on the tread. I remember thinking what an arrogant prick.
So I'm on the treadmill now and I begin to press buttons but nothing is working. I'm thinking the power's off so I go to turn on the button but it's not coming on. I look to the side of me and see my man silently laughing to himself. Well more so smiling and his teeth were perfection. Straight, brilliantly white and perfect size. I loved the way his eyes chinked too when he smiled. I ask him what his problem was. He strode over to me, each of his chocolate arms swinging like loaded guns. He came to stand next to me and said, 'well what I was going to tell you, before you happened to inform me of your status, was that this thread isn't working. But you also told me to move and so what a lady wants, a lady gets." He said blinking his gorgeous brown eyes at me. I gripped my teeth because

I knew I had to apologise and I hate apologising. He walked away after that and continued with his own workout to my annoyance. I'm used to getting attention and he wasn't giving it, made me want him more..."

As she recites this story, I wondered where the 'funny' part was. I wasn't totally sure that she'd already said it and I could tell she hadn't finished so I let her continue.

"Yeah, so I go gym a few more times after that. Didn't see him again until this one time I go with Cyan..."

She pauses. It feels like an eternity before she starts again. I'm wondering why that is again, I let her continue.

"...So we're both on a treadmill, side by side. I still haven't seen 'handsome' in a few weeks and I'm always anticipating his arrival. So I'm talking to her about her music thing and how she needs to be more proactive with booking events and getting it started because she wants to take off and that, then he walks in. I see him first. Cyan's head is down fiddling with the buttons on the treadmill to make it go faster. He walks past us to go to the dumbbell area. I had told Cyan about him briefly before so once he entered I was excited about finally showing her who he was. I nudged her to get her attention, whispered, 'that's him' and pointed behind us. She looked around,"

China rolled her eyes at this point, so I knew something unexpected was coming.

""Ty?" she said as she saw him. He turned around and looked at her and asked what she was doing here, coming to over to where we were. I was annoyed, this damn girl knew everyone. I was half hoping it wasn't someone she'd been with, knowing her track record it could have been. I was waiting to hear the story of how they knew one another. Biting my cheek, dreading what I thought

being an actual reality. They conversed about what she was doing in this gym, how it wasn't local for her, etc. etc. That's when I had enough. I needed to know how they knew each other. I asked, 'So how do you two know one another then?' They laughed together, Cyan slapped his arm. I looked at her straight-faced. 'Tyrone's my cousin!'."

So China was seeing her best friends' cousin, while her best friend was seeing her boyfriend. I wondered if Cyan knew about the relationship between them. I decided to ask.

"Okay, so does Cyan know about your relationship with her cousin, Tyrone?"

China looked at me and a sly smile spread across her face.

Cyan Imogen Brown

"Cyan, tell me a bit about your relationship with China. How would you describe your friendship?"

"She's my main girl! We've been friends since I don't even know when. She's that one chick you go to for realness. She puts everything into perspective for you. I guess you can say she's my main motivator, always pushing me to succeed. I think we got that relationship at school, she was always busy striving to achieve and it kind of rubs off on me. I'm not naturally that way inclined, but she's so focused it makes me want to do more too. Like, I follow her lead. And she's strong. She's been there for me through rough times – not necessarily been the best at being emotional, but I have enough emotions for the two of us which is why I think she's my best friend. She helps me look beyond my emotions and see the problem and whether there are any solutions. I remember this one time..."

Before she was about to tell me yet another story, which I didn't need to hear because I got the picture, there was something I had been meaning to ask her.

"I know before the sessions we had discussed whether or not you would like to share with others that you come to these sessions to talk with me, but as China seems to be your best-friend, do you tell her you come here?" I asked.

I had asked all of the girls and they had all said they would not like others to know.

"Hell no! We close...but nah, there are few things I want to keep to myself, just like she does...she barely tells me anything she's feeling."

I cut her off before she began to vent, I could see it coming, and asked her more about the emotional side of their friendship and how she had handled this news of her boyfriend.

Cyan thought before she spoke, for the first time.

"Now that you mention it, she hasn't really reacted to it. I mean she's never really been one to show her emotions anyway but I guess this is different. She was with him for what, 4 years and they had some kind of relationship so you'd think she'd be more cut up about it but she hasn't been much, or I haven't seen her in that way anyway."

"Given your relationship to him also, has that affected your relationship with her?"

Again, she sat and thought. *"You know what in all honesty, she rarely spoke about him and that made it easier for me to see him behind her back. It was as though they weren't actually together. That was until I'd see him calling her or see them hit up events together. She never really came to me with problems they had and if she did, it was followed by what she had already planned to do about it. I just used to sit and listen."*

"And did you or have you shared about your feelings about him?"

"I have been upset but to be honest I haven't seen her much. She's kept herself busy and I guess that's her way of coping."

"Do you think she has a network of people around her who supports her?"

"Maybe. Not that she'll really rely on them for help though. She's really independent. I remember Tyrone, my cousin, telling me the first time he met her, how she was and it didn't surprise me at all."

I was happy that Cyan had brought up this cousin of hers.

"So Tyrone, your cousin, knows China?"

"Yeah, they met at the gym."

"Oh, so they're gym buddies?"

"I wouldn't put it like that, no."

"So how would you put it?"

Cyan scrunched up her face, as though she wasn't sure herself how to put it. But I was intrigued by the answer she gave me.

Phoebe Roberts

"So tell me about the last time you spent with him. What was that like?"

"He came over to mine. It was quite late, as it usually is. He was very tired but that's what I liked when we'd just sit and chill till he'd fall asleep. Sounds boring I know but I just liked being in his presence half the time."

"What did you guys talk about?"

"He mainly spoke about his day, often vented to be about the nonsense he'd have to put up with at work and that."

"Did he speak about any of the people he was working with?"

I sounded like a detective, but I was greatly curious as to how Phoebe had no idea about these other girls. Whether it was due to his deliberate attempt to keep her from knowing, or whether she was extremely naive or just didn't want to accept that fact that there may be others as she was so loyal.

"Yeah, as it goes. There was this one artist he used to talk about a lot."

"Go on."

"I can't really remember her name, erm..."

I sat and watched as she racked her brains trying to recall the name. I knew she was talking about Cyan but didn't want to give too much away as to what I knew.

Finally, she remembered and pronounced Cyan's real name.

"Yeah, he used to talk about her a lot."

"What kind of things did he used to say?"

"That she was annoying." She laughed.

But that outburst surprised me. From what Cyan had said, they were 'best friends' so how could he possibly have found her annoying?

"In what ways did he say she was annoying?"

"Like, she was too much. Always wanted to do this and do that and spoke too much. She didn't like to listen either. There was loads of stuff. She was always late for sessions and when she did get there she either had no clue of the song they had just been working on or she'd get easily distracted. He also said she was too emotional too."

"Did he - or do you - have an idea of how she may have felt towards him, just in terms of their working relationship – do you think she may have felt the same way about him or not?"

I wanted to see if Phoebe had any inkling that something more may have gone on between them. I also wasn't sure if this guy had presented Cyan in that way to deter any thoughts from Phoebe's mind that something may be going on. Or, whether he genuinely felt that way about her and that Cyan had literally been exaggerating the whole thing.

But then why would Cyan need to lie to me about that? Especially as he was her best friends' boyfriend. It wasn't something you'd usually confess to unless it was true. Plus, not only did Cyan have stories for days (okay, a lot of them were over the top), but still one doesn't just create specific and vivid events out of thin air like that. Robyn was his main confidant and what he'd told her was in line with what Cyan had told me but in stark contrast to what I was now hearing from Phoebe. Clearly, he had been lying to Phoebe.

"He told me once that he thinks she may fancy him a little but that she's quite a flirty character anyway so it could just be her vibe. I don't know. He said, even if he wasn't with me, he still wouldn't go there though,"

"Did he say why?"

"Yeah, he said it's because she's too much and she acts too much like a child. He likes his women to be somewhat mature. I don't know."

But I did know. He was definitely trying to keep Phoebe in the dark as much as possible, trying to paint a picture that was so far from the truth just to keep his little secrets, secrets. The more I learned about him the less I liked him. But still, that didn't mean he didn't deserve what happened to him.

Robyn McKenzie

I planned to quiz Robyn more about Cyan, as she seemed to be the most interesting character to get information from so far. Cyan was disliked by 2 out of 4 of the girls; clearly, she was highly dysfunctional.

"I know she's not one of your favourite people but can you tell me more about Cyan. What did he used to tell you about her?"

"Argh," She said with the deepest annoyance, *"He found her sexy. I can't lie, she's quite dynamic and so is her style. I can guess why guys would be attracted to her. She has got the full package, although she did used to annoy him sometimes,"*

"Oh, in what sense?"

"Like sometimes she could be, 'too much' he'd say. Sometimes he'd like it but other times it would, I don't know, annoy him?" Robyn was trying to find the best word to use and I guess that was it. It was the same thing he had told Phoebe. *"She didn't always have it together which annoyed him because he doesn't like that. She was disorganised and too carefree."* She concluded before pausing to think.

I knew what Robyn was thinking; she was about to say what I was going to ask, so I asked anyway.

"Do you think if it wasn't for this side of her personality, that he would have left China for Cyan?"

"Not going to even lie, yes. I think so. I mean according to him they got on like a house on fire. He spoke more about her than he did about China, but there was this level of respect he had for China;

like she was his first lady. She was the one he could see himself settling down with, getting married to and starting a family with. She had it together, she was ambitious. She knew what she wanted and was going to get it. He liked that and wanted to keep that. But then on the flip side, Cyan was the one he'd have the most fun with and they had their music passion in common. And from what I know she was good in bed too." Robyn sighed.

She had done so much analysing that she was even tired from it all. But I was grateful for all that she had shared. I knew she felt defeatist because he hadn't felt that way about her.

"How did you feel about him Robyn?" With that question, she burst into tears.

I waited for her to calm down. It was obvious that her feelings for him were a lot stronger than the other females. Perhaps it was because she had known him the longest and knew him better than the rest of them.

"He never knew how I felt about him. Not that it would have made any difference anyway. He was so wrapped up with these girls; he would never have had time for me anyway. And I know, if he's cheating on the one he classed as his 'perfect woman'...."

I wasn't sure who she was referring to here: China or Cyan, but I didn't bother to ask; it wasn't important.

"...then he would have cheated on me too; not that it didn't feel like that anyway."

"Was there ever a time where you thought your friendship would become something more?"

"No never. He just didn't see me like that. From day one he was infatuated with China. It was always China this, China that. Then

when it wasn't China, it was Cyan this and Cyan that. It was never me."

"Does that affect how you feel about what happened to him?"

"I would never wish that on him. I just knew he could do better than those girls. I knew him better than he knew himself. I could have made him happy if only he'd let me."

"So, what about you? Your love life?" This question wasn't really protocol but I was curious. I was sure a girl as caring as she came across would have, at the very least, one admirer. I doubted that she had a boyfriend because it was quite clear that all of her attention was focused on this best friend of hers.

"I don't have one." She said blankly.

"There is no one you know who is interested in you, or that you are talking to who may have a liking towards you?"

"Not that I know of..."

I could tell that she was trying to be humble but the way her voice trailed off let me know there was someone there. Maybe not someone she regarded as a potential but someone there.

"Are there other guys on the scene, in whatever capacity, or was it just him?"

"Well, there's this one guy. I wouldn't say it's like 'that' between us. He's just a friend really."

"Okay, tell me a bit about him."

"He's a sweetboy."

"How do you mean?"

"Like, he's quite soft, he's caring and considerate but like to the extreme. I don't really like how much he seems to care for me, it's a bit uncomfortable."

"So he's not really the aggressive type then?"

"No."

I paused to allow her time to think more about his qualities. To see if there were things about him that she did like.

She started up again, *"I suppose he is there for me. Like when I want someone to talk and vent to, he's there to listen. I guess I like that. But I always wonder why he seems to like me so much."*

"Why?"

"Because..."

She was reluctant to tell me what she was thinking. It probably was her being self-critical.

"Because I mean, who would want me?"

She wasn't actually asking me, it was more of a rhetorical question but I wanted to break that down.

"How does he make you feel when you're talking to him?"

"Special."

"Isn't that a good thing?"

"Yeah, I just...I just don't see him that way."

"That's fair enough. Does he know you feel that way?"

"Yeah, I mean he knows how I feel about 'him'."

"Oh, so you've spoken to him about your 'best friend'?"

"Oh yeah. Not so much at the start but recently I had been offloading to him a lot."

I glanced at the clock, our time was up but there was one more question I wanted to ask her.

"What did you tell him?"

China Rhea Redson

I had been looking forward to meeting with China again. The last time she was here I had asked her whether or not Cyan knew about the secret relationship she was having with her cousin. Her answer had been, "No."

I asked her how they had managed to keep it a secret.

"We had an attraction. It was simply physical. I wanted him because he wasn't interested. He started off as an exciting hobby. I enjoyed going to the gym to get his attention more than actually working out. Then he'd eventually come over to give me tips on my workout and we began working out together. I flirted with him like mad. I knew he got the hint he was just playing hard to get. But he was great to talk to as well. He made sense as a man and so that level of attraction just went up. Then one day I just decided to be direct and tell him I wanted him. I guess he liked that."

"So what happened with your boyfriend, didn't he say anything about him?"

"We agreed that what we had was something special. I told him I didn't want to finish it with my boyfriend and that I didn't want him to find out. He was funny about it at first but then agreed to it, on the condition that I couldn't tell Cyan. He hasn't ever really said why to be honest, I guess it's because she has a big mouth and he didn't want his family involved in his business."

"Why didn't you want to end your relationship to be with Tyrone?"

"We'd been together for a long time. He made sense in my life. We had spoken about a future together. I wasn't about to give that all

up for a guy I felt sexually attracted to and had no idea where it was going."

"You said that it's more than just a physical attraction though; you said that he 'makes sense'."

"Yeah, in the way that only a few guys make sense in this life. He had his shit together, which is rare these days and he was good at conversation as well as being physically fit. We didn't have the history as I did with 'him'."

"So you wanted to be sure about him?"

I was trying to establish their relationship. Why he was her bit on the side really, because from what she was saying it didn't just sound like it was just a sexual attraction, it sounded like she had feelings for him.

"At first it was just about sex. It was. But then I liked his personality so I wanted to keep him around. That was it really. He gave me the time that my boyfriend didn't, with him being in that goddamn studio all the time, I never really got to see him and I got used to it. So, Ty was there for me when I just needed to offload."

I was slowly getting it. She wanted to have her cake and eat it too. Just like her boyfriend. Probably why they were such a good match! But I wondered how close she actually was to Cyan and whether or not she actually trusted her as a friend.

I had asked Cyan her view of their friendship but I hadn't yet asked China.

"Tell me a bit about your friendship with Cyan. How did you two become friends and so close?"

"I don't really know how we became so close, to be honest. We were friends in school, in the same form and she was put to sit next

to me because her behaviour wasn't the greatest and they (the teachers) thought that I would be a positive influence on her I guess. She annoyed me at first, she's quite chatty and attention seeking so she'd try and distract me a lot in lessons but soon after our mock exams in Year 10, she realised that education was important– she failed and I didn't so she asked for my help. I mean she was capable, she just needed to focus more in lessons and so I agreed to be her 'study-buddy'."

"How comes you wanted to help her?"

"She was funny when she wasn't distracting me. She was the girl you'd go to for jokes and gossip. She just kind of just clung on."

That made sense. China was talking almost as though she didn't particularly care whether or not Cyan was her friend. She seemed to be just someone she had there, who needed her more than she needed her. Now was time for the real question.

"How did Cyan feel when you got with your boyfriend?"

China thought for a few moments, as though her mind was travelling back in time trying to recall their first interaction.

Cyan Imogen Brown

I had known that Cyan didn't know about China and Tyrone's secret relationship from my last session with her. I could tell from the face she gave me that if anything she wouldn't have suspected a thing going on between them. She told me how they didn't get along, well from when she observed them together, the times she followed China to the gym.

"She didn't seem to even give him any notice when we were all there and when he used to come over to talk to us she was quite rude to him...well I say rude but that's China being China, she can come across rude to people who don't really know her. They must have barely exchanged two words between them."

"Didn't you think that was a bit odd given that she had been telling you about him before you found out he was your cousin?" I asked, remembering the tiny detail that China had told me about having told Cyan about the 'sexy guy who attended her gym'.

Cyan shifted in her seat, as though an uncomfortable thought had entered her mind, *"Not until you just asked me that actually. No. I guess me being related to him must have put her off him!"* She said laughing but I could see that her own thought had slightly offended her.

I decided to change the subject, "How often did you go gym with her?"

"Not that often. I didn't really go gym, most of my time was spent with him in the studio and I go for jogs and runs to keep my fitness up. But as China is always busy, going gym with her sometimes is the only way to really spend any time with her."

I could see that their friendship was severely lopsided; with Cyan doing most of the work. I figured that was probably why she didn't feel so bad sleeping with her boyfriend. It could be that Cyan didn't really regard China as a friend and so felt better about her actions. I didn't find it strange that Cyan had no idea about China and her cousin, Tyrone. She came across fickle and largely in her own world so it wasn't a surprise that she saw and accepted things at face value.

We spoke briefly about her work and what music she was currently working on in the studio, to break up the conversation a little, before coming back to talk about the night we were here to discuss.

"So tell me about this party. How much of it did you know about and were you due to attend?"

"I knew about the party. China had told me about it, I remember because I was irritated that he didn't tell me, not that I would have gone anyway...I literally hate seeing them together...not that I'm ever going to see it again now."

Cyan put her head down, the memory of grief slowly coming back to her.

I gave her a moment to compose herself. I wondered if she loved him, properly loved him and desired him to leave her to be with him or whether she was content being his thing on the side. I asked just that.

"They worked well together. I knew I couldn't give him what she could; stability, loyalty and reliability. I loved him but I couldn't be his everything."

Phoebe Roberts

I was curious to know what Phoebe's life was like when he wasn't around. So far, she had told me that she worked at a GP practice and that was it really. Hardly an interesting social life but he had to do more than just work and home. What was her home life like? I wondered.

"So the times when you didn't see him, what would you do with yourself?" I asked her, trying to draw information out of her, which was often a chore.

"I wouldn't really do much, just chill, watch reality TV shows or do some cooking. Other than that I wouldn't really do much."

"So you don't really do much outdoorsy type things, like swimming, bowling, cinema?" I refused to believe that a girl this young and this pretty, just sat indoors all day doing nothing.

She sighed, as though she was often asked this and was getting fed up of it.

"Honestly, I'm the be-at-home type; my brother and I are quite similar in that respect."

Now we were getting somewhere, she had a brother; something which had come up before, but I hadn't asked about.

"Tell me a bit more about your brother. What is he like, what is your relationship like?"

"He is older than me by two years, he can be quiet but then I guess that is because he doesn't really talk to me that much. He has this

thing where he thinks that by not telling me certain things, he is protecting me!

"So he is quite protective over you, would you say?"

"Oh yes. I mean, he's my big brother and he won't let me forget it.

"So would you say that you had a good relationship?"

"It depends what you mean. We get along really well when he isn't being all territorial about what I'm doing and the friends I keep. But I don't really tell him about things anymore. I used to but now he spends most of his time in his room online."

"Would you say he is quite a social person?"

"He's not that social in person, he's more of a social networking-on-the-computer type. I think he has the most followers on twitter or something. He has a good social media personality but not really in person."

I was now clearer about him. From what Phoebe was telling me, he was someone you would not really notice at a social event but was well known on social media platforms. I had heard about these kinds of people. They were able to create a persona online, to people who didn't really know the real them, and literally be anyone they wanted to be. If he looked anything like Phoebe, then he was quite an attractive guy. Light-skinned with wavy black hair, I imagined.

"Does he have an alias? An online name that he goes by or do people simply know him as…?" I remembered that Phoebe hadn't actually told me his name, not that I cared to know. She helped me out,

"His name is Marcus but people call him Magz so I guess that is a part of his twitter name. It's @MagnetoDaGreat or something."

"Strange." I wasn't sure why he would call himself that; sounded a bit egotistical. But of course, I didn't know him.

"Yeah, I don't know. I'm blocked from following him. He's quite secretive. Even with mum and dad. It's weird, it's as though I don't really know the true him anymore."

I felt sad for Phoebe. I thought perhaps this was why she seemed quite introverted and to herself. I figured that she once had a close relationship with her brother but through their teenage years, they had drifted apart. Perhaps the lifestyle he adopted meant that he had to put on this new persona or perhaps he felt, as he got older, the need to protect his sister from the world as he knew it and the only way he knew how was through distancing himself from her. She also didn't seem to know anything much about him either. It was as though he was a lodger in her house that looked like her and shared the same parents. I was sure she was exaggerating about how much of a recluse he was, but I had to take her word for it.

Robyn McKenzie

I reminded Robyn of what we had discussed in our last session. We had spoken about Cyan and China, what she thought of them and how that had affected her relationship with him. Then, we had gone on to talk about her own love life and this guy she had been offloading to.

I had asked her what she had told him, just before our session had come to a close and she had taken so long to think about what she had said, (I think it was more to do with wanting to share than actually trying to remember), that I suggested she share next time, if she wanted to.
But I had been curious about what she had told him. I wasn't sure why, I think it was because it seemed strange to me that she would share something so deep and personal with a complete stranger. I was more curious about what this guy was like that she felt able to talk about someone else with him.

"So, do you remember what we spoke about last time, when I asked you what you told him?"

"Oh yeah, I told him about my best friend. I know I shouldn't have probably but I felt it best to just let him know my situation."

"And what is your situation?"

"That I had feelings for my best friend."

She said it so bluntly, which I found weird because she always seemed so in touch with her feelings.

"What was his reaction? What did he say about it?" I was wondering how a guy who clearly had interest took knowing that the person he was interested in, had feelings for someone else and why he decided to stay and listen.

"He just asked me questions really, based on things I would tell him."

"Okay, things like what?"

"So when we first began talking, I didn't realise that he was interested in me. We had good banter, he made me laugh and so we joked about things we both found funny more often. So it was only when I had a low mood and he would pick up on it, that I would offload. He made me feel comfortable enough to share, I don't how or why as he was a complete stranger but then again maybe that's why. Maybe I liked the elusiveness of him not knowing me or my life and the people I'd speak about so it made it easier to share."

She paused to contemplate on what she had just said, as though she was only now worrying that maybe she had been a bit too open with him.

"He knew all about him, our friendship. How I felt about him with all of his girls and other things too."

"What did he have to say about it?"

"He seemed genuinely concerned. He told me how from what I'd tell him, that he didn't like him and wondered why I called him my best friend when he clearly wasn't a nice guy or seem to have any respect for me or my feelings."

"What made him say he wasn't a nice guy?"

"Because of all the girls he had on the go. I told him about China and Cyan...wasn't sure of the last one's name and as I didn't know much about her, I couldn't share that much. But he was the kind of

guy that didn't like boys who played girls. He had a thing about it. He felt that he must have known that I had feelings for him but still decided to share with me his business."

"What did you say in response to all what he said?"

"I just defend him, as I always do. No one really understands... understood, sorry, our relationship anyway, so I just didn't expect him to get it. Like, I knew that he wasn't what you'd call a 'good' guy but he was always there for me when I needed him and to me, that meant a lot."

Robyn told me more about her and this guy's new budding friendship, how she felt that he was beginning to turn into her best friend these days and that she wasn't totally sure whether or not she liked him in 'that' way. She also told me that he hadn't actually met him in real life...

China Rhea Redson

It had been a few weeks until I saw China again. She had been busy. Well, too busy to come to see me. She had 'a hundred and one' things she had to do for some event, she had been organising, and just 'didn't have the time'. I think she felt that she was more here for me than for herself. She was, in one sense. I was still trying to piece together this complicated story of their lives and she was a key fixture in this puzzle. Her information was invaluable, not just because of what her status had been in his life, but also because of who else she was connected to.

I had asked her whether she knew how Cyan had felt about the start of her relationship with her actual boyfriend and she had said,

"She wasn't really that concerned. I didn't really bring them around one another. It was either I was spending time with him or I was spending time with her. I didn't really see the need to spend time with the two of them together. I felt that they would probably end up killing each other. Cyan has a way of being annoying, and I can barely stand it, I'm sure he would have become much more annoyed."

'*On the contrary*', I thought to myself. She was too busy talking to notice I had a smirk on my face, one that I removed as soon as she next focused her attention towards me. I could tell that she had no idea from what she was saying of the possibility that he could potentially have been seeing someone else, let alone her friend.

"Well do you know what he thought about Cyan? Did her name ever come up in conversation?"

I knew the answer but I just wanted to ask for clarification.

"*No.*" She replied. Just as I thought.

"What do you think Cyan thought about him? Did you two ever discuss him, or did she give an opinion on him?"

China paused, momentarily to think about what I had asked her. It was clear from her inquisitive facial expression that either she didn't remember ever having a conversation about him with her, or that she had no idea how Cyan felt because they actually never did discuss him.

However, it turned out China could remember conversations she had with Cyan. She was merely wondering whether they had been positive or negative.

"*I remember having had an argument with him and was venting to Cyan about it, something I rarely did because we rarely argued, but she didn't seem at all that bothered. She just dismissed it as though all guys were like that and told me that I was too beautiful to allow any boy take the piss...just the usual girl-to-girl things. She didn't seem to ever really take him in as a person. I can be quite secretive, especially about my private life so she barely knew anything about our relationship really.*"

I found it amazing how he had been so intimate with two girls who were so close and had got away with one of them not knowing. He was clearly great at playing this game. Either that or these two girls were extremely blind and naive.

Cyan Imogen Brown

"How did you manage to keep up this front to China, Cyan?" I had to ask. I couldn't remember if I had asked before or not but I needed to understand and I currently did not. I was trying to understand why someone would possibly go behind their friend's back in this way.

"Well, she didn't respect him. She didn't love him or appreciate him. Not in the way I did. Plus there was something about the way he was with me. The way he looked at me. The way he showed how much he desired me. It was sexy and extremely hard to avoid. We never planned it. It just happened all the time. Most times I wasn't even thinking about China. I was in the moment. Just with him."

I understood to a point. She was extremely self-involved. I could see it in her actions. In the way she spoke about herself. As if the only thing that really matters was herself. Yes, she had an appearance of caring for others but it was a facade. If it implicated her in any way then she would ensure that her own feelings came first. This childish attitude she had towards things also worked in her favour. It was almost like it was hard to see how she couldn't see the world through 'adult eyes'. She was still very much a child at heart. Living from one moment to the next, with no regard for others; their thoughts or feelings.

"So all of the times you were with him, you didn't think of how China might have felt or been feeling?" I quizzed her.

"To be honest, no. I didn't think about her at all when I was with him. It was either all about music or about the sex. Nothing else was really topic of conversation. We liked it like that. It was as though we were two other people."

Yes, definitely living in her dream world. She probably thought that this was all a game to her. I wondered if she had anything to do with his death unknowingly...

Phoebe Roberts

I never really got much from Phoebe. The last time I had seen her, she had told me about her brother who she was not all that close to. He was two years older, protective and secretive.

I was struggling to understand how he was protective over her when they seemed to barely have any kind of relationship. I wondered if it was just her perception or whether it was just something he felt he had to be, being the older brother.

"Are there any incidents where Marcus has been overprotective over you?" I asked her, trying to get to the bottom of their relationship.

"Just in school. There were quite a few guys in his year who liked me. They were popular guys, not like him and so they often teased him about getting with me. He hated it."

"Did he do anything about it?"

"He had a fight one time with the main guy Francis. I remember that because Francis had tried to flirt with me in front of him and he didn't like it."

"What was his problem with boys in his school year liking you?" I didn't really understand the problem. Yes, she was younger and yes these guys were probably just having a laugh but it wasn't as though anything was actually happening. I still couldn't understand.

"Francis had a girlfriend. Marcus hated that he was trying it on with me when he already had a girlfriend."

But still I couldn't understand why that would cause Marcus to want to fight him, "Okay, but why did that make him so angry, he got into a physical fight with this boy?"

Eventually, Phoebe got there.

"Well, my dad left us because he found another woman. I think that affected Marcus way more than he would care to be open with. Since then he's the man of the house and he feels in some way, that it is his duty to protect both me and mum from guys like that."

Finally, we got to the root of it all. "So did you tell him about this guy you were dating?" I asked her, anticipating her answer.

Robyn McKenzie

"So Robyn, last time you were here, you told me that you hadn't met this guy in real life?"

"Yeah..."

"Well, isn't that a bit dangerous, you know sharing personal information with someone you've not actually met. What if he is not who he says he is."

"Well we actually know a few of the same people. Funnily enough one of my boys knows of him. I showed him a picture and he told me he used to play ball with him."

"Ahh so you've got a picture of him. Can I see?"

While Robyn fumbled around in her bag, trying to grab her phone so that she could show me, I was curious to think how strange it was that she was able to trust people so quickly. I found it quite dangerous and thought that it was a bit out of character for Robyn to do so also.

She passed me the phone and instantly there was something about him that looked strangely familiar...

China Rhea Redson

There was something different about China this time she came to see me. She was quieter than usual and barely said two words when she first sat down. If I didn't know her, I would have said she was almost, upset.

"China, how are you doing?"

"I'm alright." A blatant lie.

"You don't really seem yourself?"

"Well, that would be the case if you just found out your best friend had been sleeping with your man!" She said in an angry huff. Though, she sounded more irritated and angry at having exposed her inner thoughts than at her disclosure.

I was shocked. I hadn't anticipated her finding out, especially now that he was dead. It was as though now that he wasn't around to cause trouble, there was nothing to share. But I was wrong.

I wasn't sure I wanted to know all of the details, but of course, I had to ask...

"How did you feel about what she was saying?"

"We were arguing about something random, completely forgot what it was and I must have said something that pressed her buttons...sometimes I can be a bit flippant and she doesn't like it...she just exploded at me, started venting at me...getting really hyper and I was telling her to calm down and relax but it was somehow giving her more energy. It was strange. Telling me that I'm this and that, that I think I'm too nice and I'm not above people

in the way I think I am...all of this crap and nonsense basically. Then I asked her what she was talking about because as far as I was concerned she was chatting shit. So I told her who I was, that I wasn't taking shit from anyone and that no one could embarrass me or make me feel like shit. Then she started saying all this about how there were things I don't know and that's when she blurted it out... how, 'I'm not the perfect girl I think I am otherwise my man wouldn't have slept with her multiple times'... saying that I've been taking shit for ages and that they'd been sleeping together behind my back for ages."

"What was your initial reaction?" I asked. I was a little amused as I had no idea what a girl like China would have done in that predicament. I mean it simply wasn't something that happened to someone like her.

Cyan Imogen Brown

I had been anticipating seeing Cyan ever since my session with China. I needed to get the other side's version of events and there was no one who could tell me better than Cyan herself.

"How are things?" I began. Everything that China had told me was confidential so I couldn't just blurt out any information that suggested I already knew about her fall out with China. I didn't have to push further either.

"Basically, yeah, I told China that I was sleeping with him before he died. It was in the heat of an argument...sometimes she can be really mean, like condescending, and I just wanted to put her back in her place, you know; let her know that she isn't this great girl that she thinks she is."

"Well, how did she take it?"

I wanted to understand Cyan's perception of China's reaction more than anything. I wanted to see if she was deep down a considerate person, or if she was as self-concerned as she often came across in our sessions.

Sighing, *"She didn't say anything at first. She was just staring at me blankly. Then she started asking me all these questions, like how it started, when we had time to do this...but she never asked why."*

That mainly interested me, as I knew China well enough to know, by asking those questions, she was trying to find the logic behind it; more so than actually bringing her feelings into the situation. Cyan was the opposite, clearly moved by emotions - particularly as a defence mechanism - and it was quite obvious that she was offended China hadn't reacted in the way that she'd hoped. She'd wanted to hurt China, but as it seemed as though she hadn't, she was annoyed about it.

"Why was it important to you that she asked 'why'? Wouldn't you want to know all the details too?" I asked.

"It's not that it's important but I figured, why be concerned with all the 'hows' and 'wheres'? That doesn't change what happened and why it did. Doesn't it make more sense to understand the reason behind it?"

"Perhaps she already knew." Was all I could reply.

Phoebe Roberts

The last time I had seen Phoebe, I had asked if her brother had known about her relationship and her answer had been 'no' and to be completely honest, I wasn't that surprised. I mean who would tell their older, overprotective brother that they were seeing a guy, especially with his track record with beating boys up for even talking to her?

"Would you have ever told him?" I doubted that she would, but I still had to ask.

"Yes, if it got more serious, I would've had to tell him sooner or later."

I remembered something she had told me.

"You said that he used to come to see you at yours sometimes, did your brother not ever meet him when he came round."

"Nah, my brother was either working late or always in his room. We were careful, well I was anyway. I know that sounds weird, but they literally never bumped into each other."

In my head, something was telling me that she was wrong, that they probably had met on the landing, on the way to the toilet or something; it just seemed too strange to have not.

"Did he know your brother?"

"Nope, he didn't know my brother and I wasn't actually that surprised"

"How do you mean?"

"Well, my brother isn't well-known or that respected. He's quiet, doesn't have much confidence in himself and as far as I know, he doesn't have many friends, he doesn't even know how to talk to girls!"

I pondered on that statement. I didn't know her brother, didn't know anyone who knew him or so I thought.

After my session with Phoebe, something sent a shiver down my spine. She smiled as she was leaving, and there was something about her smile that bothered me. Not in a horrible way, I just found it weirdly familiar.

Robyn McKenzie

"How's this guy of yours?"

"To be honest, he's been a bit distant from me recently. I think he's giving me time to grieve."

I nodded in agreement with her presumption. She was probably right. There was still something familiar about this guy but I couldn't quite place what it was.

"Well, when was the last time you spoke to him?"

She looked to the ceiling as she tried to recall the last conversation they had, in her mind.

"I think it was just before the incident."

"What was the conversation about? If you don't mind telling me." This was becoming much more ominous.

"Well, we spoke for ages that time. I had been crying because I had found out who the last girl he was messing with was. I was in shock because she wasn't someone I would put him with, she was so boyish even though she's very pretty; I just didn't think it was his type. I was angry at having been there for him, having all these pent-up feelings when all this time he was messing around with her. Like what was wrong with me? Why her and not me? It didn't make sense to me!" She said with tears free-falling down her cheeks.

I had two questions.

The first, "How did you find out who she was?"

I was quite unnerved that she knew of Phoebe outside of her being one of the girls he was seeing.

"I went round to his house. Went to see his mum, you know, she's like Aunty, and she told me that there were a few things I had lent him he was going to give me back that week...she had left them on his bed and couldn't face going into his room so I went there to get them. That's when I saw the card. It was on the floor, peeking out from under his bed. I was surprised it was there because he never kept things like that lying around. I knew he never let Cyan into his house and that China barely went to his anyway but still, he would have kept that hidden. She had printed out a picture of them and stuck it on and had printed her name at the bottom, 'With love Phoebe'. I wanted to vomit."

My second question was how she knew her, and apparently they had gone to the same acting school for a few months. Phoebe had left because, according to Robyn, *'she had no personality'* but I think it probably just wasn't for her. Apparently, they had got along alright while they were there, but the abrupt nature of Phoebe's departure and not saying goodbye to Robyn was enough for her to be in Robyn's bad books forever and now there was this.

"So you told this guy you were talking to about it, what did you tell him?"

"I told him that I had found out who the other girl was, how I knew her and how I couldn't understand how and why they had even got together. I was just venting to him really, he's good to talk to."

"What did he say in response?"

"He said what he usually says... how this guy is a waste of my energy and why would I even want to be with a guy who clearly

doesn't rate me, etc... I know he's right but I couldn't help the way I felt in total honesty."

It was clear this was what Robyn needed to hear, not that she was actually hearing it, however. I was glad that she was talking to someone about it, instead of bottling up her emotions at least. Nevertheless, at the same time, I was concerned about just how much information she was giving out to a complete stranger. I had to ask...

"What is his name?"

China Rhea Redson

I had asked China what her initial reaction was to Cyan's outburst, intrigued as to how she handled the situation...

"I was confused. I mean I just wanted to know how and where this took place and how I never knew of this. I couldn't believe he would do this to me either, I mean I made it clear that he would live to regret it if he ever cheated on me. I just found it a bit insensitive of her to bring this up after his death too. She had this whole time to tell me and she didn't but she called herself my friend. The whole thing made no sense."

With Cyan's voice in my head, I asked, "Was that it? Were you not concerned with the why?"

"Why is that important? They did it, it doesn't change anything, it is done now so why is not going to help anything."

"Yes, but don't you think it would help prevent it from happening again with someone else in the future?"

She paused to consider my question and I thought I had finally gotten through to her but I was wrong. She was so strong-minded in her own convictions that she couldn't bear to think of any other viewpoint but her own.

"I won't find another man who will cheat on me, let alone with my best friend. It just won't happen, I'm better than that and I deserve a guy who knows my worth."

I wanted to bury my head in my hands. I knew what she was saying was probably her truth but was it realistic? I didn't want to burst her bubble so I ignored her response and moved past it.

"So you had no idea the two of them were seeing each other?"

I wasn't completely surprised; she acted as though he was someone she knew rather than someone she was actually seeing.

"None." She said, looking at her acrylic nails as though bored of the current conversation.

I couldn't help but think that she didn't care about anyone but herself. That she hadn't been invested in the relationship with him and so this was all just a bit of a waste of time for her. She sure was acting like it.

In the back of my mind, I knew I would probably get more out of Cyan, regarding the aftermath of their friendship, than I was getting from China but I knew it was important for the two of them to discuss this so that it would not happen again.

"I think it is important that you two actually have a proper conversation about this. Do you not feel betrayed, that your trust has been abused?" I tried, trying to get China to think about the bigger picture.

China paused, considering my question. Finally, she put her hands down and looked me in my eyes.

"You know what, you're right. I do need to know why. She needs to explain herself."

Cyan Imogen Brown

"So how were things with China after you confessed to cheating with her boyfriend?" I jumped straight in, as Cyan liked it that way. She wasn't the type to beat around the bush and do small talk.

"I texted her asking her how she is. I thought when I told her, she would have blown up at me but she didn't so I wasn't sure how we left things. I would have rather her shout, scream, tell me I'm dead to her or something so that I knew where I stood in our friendship but she just replied saying that she would like to meet up and talk about it."

As Cyan spoke about the situation, it became more evident to me that she was so hopeful of their friendship going back to how it was. I couldn't understand it. She had cheated with her friend's boyfriend, who was now dead, and she figured that the two of them would be able to sit down and work things out soon. She needed more help than I could give. I was almost certain that their friendship was over but I still encouraged her to meet up.

"Alright, I'll meet her and tell her about everything properly, with no fighting or arguing and see what she says. She's my best friend at the end of the day so I'm sure she'll forgive me eventually...I mean she wasn't really even that serious about their relationship."

I couldn't even bring myself to nod to her statement. Cyan lived in her own world with her own rules and I doubted she understood how her actions really affected others; I doubted she ever would, but from the last conversation I had with China she wanted Cyan to 'explain herself' and make it clear to Cyan that her actions were not okay.

Even if there was no resolution, they both needed that conversation to happen. For China to work out why this happened and hopefully understand a bit more about the situation and for Cyan to see that this wasn't something she could put a plaster over. I was certain their discussion wasn't going to go the way Cyan was hoping, just as I was sure the friendship wouldn't be salvageable.

Phoebe Roberts

The last time I had seen Phoebe, we had been talking about her brother. She had ended the session describing her relationship with men in particular. As her father wasn't an active presence in her life, since leaving the family, her brother was quite protective of her. She used that as a reason for why she wasn't too keen on telling her brother about the fact she was dating or who she was dating...

"Last time you mentioned that you didn't really want your brother to know who you were dating until it became more serious...I understand why you wouldn't want him to know you were dating but I feel as though you meant more than that?" I was pressing because I feared Phoebe knew more about this guy she was seeing than she let on.

Phoebe looked down at the floor. She shifted in the chair as though showing the struggle to get her words out.

"A few days ago I got a message from someone I used to know,"

What kind of message? I asked, interrupting her.

"A message on Instagram. She popped up as someone who would like to send me a message as I don't have her as a friend. I accepted it and there was practically an essay in the chat."

As she hesitated, I waited unsure whether or not she would continue or even wanted to but I didn't want to push her. She didn't seem comfortable as it was, and to be honest, I wasn't sure what this had to do with telling her brother about who she was seeing but I had to be patient, evidently there was more to this...

As if a light bulb had gone off in my head, I suddenly realised who she was talking about, I just had to be sure...

"Who was the message from?"

Robyn McKenzie

The moment Robyn told me the name of the guy she had been getting close to, I felt the last piece of the puzzle slot into place. The web that these girls were in was incredible. I couldn't believe so many lives were intertwined in the way they were.

It was hurtful that one person could have so much control and influence over so many people's lives and not even realise the damage they were creating. It was a strange and violent ripple effect of violence, love and jealousy.

I saw each girl in the way they had presented themselves to me, but I had also seen so much more than that. I had seen the protectiveness, the fear, the lust and the love from each one of these girls towards one another and towards the boy who was at the center of their universes.

At the same, I could see the pain, hurt and frustration through Robyn's eyes when she spoke to me. There was so much this girl had gone through and so much she was feeling. She felt A LOT. All of her emotions seemed so close to the surface, I was worried how and when they would come out. Would it be tears and sadness, anger and rage or just insane laughter? I was a bit fearful and figured that she merely needed an outlet. I allowed her to talk about whatever it was she wanted towards the end of the session and express whatever she needed to.

She began to work out, in her own mind, the pieces to the puzzle and all I could do was sit back and give her the space to do so...

Cyan Imogen Brown

Cyan came in for her final session in a troubled and emotional state. She was a shadow of her former lively colourful self, light-years away from her bubbly and carefree persona. It was strange. She slumped down in the chair and cried. I waited patiently until she had finished; it had been at least 5 minutes but eventually, she stopped. She blew her nose and looked at me with her raw, red eyes. The meet-up with China hadn't gone well then I thought.

"What's happened?" I asked, leaving my question as open as possible.

"*Everything!*" She exclaimed. This was going to be easy.

"What's everything? Can you try and be more specific?

"*I met up with China…*" She sniffed, more for effect than anything else. "*She came to the studio, she thought it would be better on my terms and I agreed because I wanted to be in a place I felt comfortable but I was wrong. It should have been in a more public place...she wouldn't have been so...so…*"

She couldn't think of the word, but I knew where she was going with it.

"*...She was so loud, so angry and she laid into me telling me how I was a horrible person, that she had put up with my crap for so long, how much of a bad friend I was and how she couldn't believe just how much I could stab her in the back like that. She just kept asking 'why?' and I couldn't give an answer…*"

I was surprised that China had gone with that approach. She was usually so controlled with expressing her emotions, in some ways not allowing others to take her power from her. I couldn't help but think that Cyan was exaggerating slightly, as she often did; seeing emotions more amplified compared to others, but I wasn't there so I could only take her word for it. The fact that Cyan couldn't give an answer told me that the penny had to have dropped. China did what she had to do and had almost forced Cyan into a corner to explain herself. I wasn't stunned or shocked that she couldn't answer. She had spent all this time acting out of emotion, I figured she knew 'why' and the 'why' was selfishness. But she wouldn't admit to that even if she was that self-aware.

Cyan continued, "*...She said how I was wrong to go behind her back and do that, regardless of what their relationship was like and said she could no longer trust me or be friends with me. That hurt the most. I never saw it like that, I know stupid me, but I didn't. I honestly just figured she didn't love or care about him like that so she wouldn't be bothered. I didn't think about it like how she presented it. I feel so bad, so awful. Not only have I lost my lover, I've lost my best friend.*" She said sobbing again.

Even though it was clear she was in emotional distress, it was so hard to feel sorry for her. I could understand though, she was so self-absorbed she couldn't see the effects of her actions on others. It was all about what she wanted and needed, no matter how it affected others. I was glad she could now see, even if it was just a little bit, just how much her actions had lost her. I hoped this experience would help her future relationships.

Phoebe Roberts

The message Phoebe had received was from Robyn telling her everything. Robyn hadn't told me that she was planning on doing that but I wasn't shocked. It seemed like something Robyn would do, acting on impulse and probably regretting it later. No doubt it was a detailed and well-written message and it was as Phoebe showed me.

"Hi Phoebe, I don't know if you remember me from acting school - Robyn? Anyway, I was friends with Jerome and happened to see a card you wrote for him...I just wanted to ask if you two were seeing each other? I know it isn't my business but I don't know if you knew that he was seeing two other girls at the same time, China and Cyan. I know this may come as a shock as it is for me but I felt you needed to know. He wasn't the person you thought he was, or I thought he was. If you don't respond to this message I completely get it, but if you do want to talk or have questions feel free to message me. I don't know everything but what I do know I can share. I feel you owe that much. R x"

As I finished reading the message, I looked up to hand Phoebe back her phone and all I could see in front of me was a lost little girl. She looked so empty, so damaged and broken. I was shocked that I didn't see it before. It wasn't hard to imagine how much this was all a shock for her and I knew she probably knew more than she wanted to by now.

I figured the truth had come out for her, the truth that had the capacity to turn her world upside down. It would take a lot more sessions of intensive therapy for her to even touch the surface of her former self.

We sat in silence while she processed, tears slowly falling from her eyes, rolling down her cheeks.

Robyn McKenzie

Robyn was the only one capable of speaking the truth and that was exactly what she did.

"I messaged Phoebe a few days after I saw that card in his room. I needed to understand... He was playing games with all of us and I wanted to know what her role in his life was in addition to the rest of us... He had China, Cyan and now Phoebe, he was meant to be my best friend and I didn't know his life at all! That's what hurts the most, seeing him play all these girls and then I'm here with feelings as well and still I wasn't anything to him. I wanted to know what Phoebe had that I didn't and you know...it wasn't even much. That wasn't even the worst of the whole thing..."

I felt that I knew what was coming. I knew what she was going to tell me and I was careful of how I was going to react to it.

"After the message went through, I did some preeing...scrolled through her pictures, just to see if I would see one of the both of them, even though I knew there probably wouldn't be just because he's careful like that...with her being one of his side-chicks, he wouldn't have his bait face just there on her social media...." She paused briefly, *"That's when I saw it."*

I caught my breath, anticipating her telling me what she had discovered.

But she didn't speak again for a long while. Instead, she sat staring into space as though she was reliving seeing what she had seen again for the first time. I gave her a few more seconds and then asked,

"What was it you saw?"

"His face. It didn't make sense at first but then it did. It was so obvious that they were brother and sister, I didn't even need to look at the caption."

I realised that was the moment she had figured it out.

It surprised me how well Robyn put everything together in her mind. I was certain she wouldn't get there or even be in denial about it being a reality, but she knew, like I did, that this was the only thing that made sense and I knew from other background information gathered that it was more than likely. Protective but violent.

"I told him everything. I even told him about Phoebe in the end, I sent him her Instagram profile to look at. How stupid am I?!" Robyn said, angry at herself for being so open and trusting with someone she barely knew. *"I had no idea... He was there for me, being a listening ear when I needed to vent... He told me I deserved better...All of it meant nothing...."* She continued, floods of tears now streaming down her face.

"It was him... it was Marcus who stabbed my bestie. He killed Jerome."

China Rhea Redson

After my last sessions with each of the girls, learning about the web of lies and deceit but eventually the truth, I reflected on the first time China came to see me and remembered her recited version of the events of that fatal night when he, her boyfriend, Jerome was murdered by Marcus, Phoebe's brother.

"...I come out of the kitchen and see Jerome in the middle of the floor holding his side. I go to him and see that there is blood on his hands... I scream at someone to call an ambulance but no one moves. I get vex and reach for the phone in my bag. This guy grabs it from me and somehow get into an argument about it...they don't want police here, blah, blah, blah. I run past him outside and knock on a neighbour's door, a couple of doors down. A woman comes to the door, looking all haggard and tired. I tell her what has happened and in her horror she lets me use her phone to call for the ambulance.
I go back to the house where the party is and see my man lying on the doorstep. By himself. I kneel down beside him to check on him he's not dead yet because I feel him still breathing, though it is slower and more shallow... he just looked like he was asleep. So now I'm mad as hell. I bang the door down, screaming and yelling. I know they can hear me inside because the music hasn't come back on, but yet no one answers. I sit down next to where he lays and place his head on my lap until the ambulance arrives but when they do come, they are too late..."

About the Author

C. Bailey-Cassell is a fiction-novel and short-story writer who has a flare for writing stories with an unexpected twist, making her readers wanting to keep turning the page.

She grew up in London, England where she still resides. In 2013, she graduated from the University of Essex with a BSc in Psychology, her favourite subject, which she says developed her passion for: 'people, personalities and the psyche'. This, along with her history of working with young adults, helped her create stories people could read and relate to; inspiring them to stretch their own imaginations.

Four Diamonds in the Rough is her debut novel.

www.ingramcontent.com/pod-product-compliance
Ingram Content Group UK Ltd.
Pitfield, Milton Keynes, MK11 3LW, UK
UKHW020236250726
13967UKWH00001B/396

9 780244 151584